To Raven Wilkinson —M.C.

G. P. PUTNAM'S SONS
Published by the Penguin Group
Penguin Group (USA) LLC
375 Hudson Street
New York, NY 10014

USA | Canada | UK | Ireland | Australia
New Zealand | India | South Africa | China
penguin.com
A Penguin Random House Company

Library of Congress Cataloging-in-Publication Data
Copeland, Misty. Firebird / Misty Copeland ; illustrated by Christopher Myers. pages cm
Summary: American Ballet Theatre soloist Misty Copeland encourages a young ballet student, with brown skin like her own, by telling her that she, too, had to learn basic steps and how to be graceful when she was starting out, and that someday, with practice and dedication, the little girl will become a firebird, too.
Includes author's note about dancers who led her to find her voice.
[1. Ballet dancing—Fiction. 2. Self-confidence—Fiction. 3. Dance—Fiction.
4. Copeland, Misty—Fiction. 5. African Americans—Fiction.] I. Title.
PZ7.C7887Fir 2014
[E]—dc23
2014008878

Manufactured in China by South China Printing Co. Ltd.
ISBN 978-0-399-16615-0
3 5 7 9 10 8 6 4 2

Design by Annie Ericsson.
Text set in Corinthian Std Bold and Mercurius CT Std Black Italic.

MISTY COPELAND

illustrated by
CHRISTOPHER MYERS

Firebird

Ballerina Misty Copeland
Shows a Young Girl How to Dance
Like the Firebird

G. P. Putnam's Sons
An Imprint of Penguin Group (USA)

the space between you and me
is longer than forever

you are the sky and clouds and air
your feet are swift as sunlight

stretching across the skyline
like the daylong sun over the horizon

me? I'm gray as rain

heavy as naptime, low as a storm pressing on rooftops

I could never hope to leap
the space between

darling child, don't you know
you're just where I started
let the sun shine on your face
your beginning's just begun

before the curtain rises
before the spotlight falls

before the fireworks of costumes
before before it all

I was a dancer just like you
a dreaming shooting star of a girl
with work and worlds ahead

there I am
sweating at the barre
I had a thousand leaps and falls
switching worn-out slippers
swift as applause

even birds must learn to fly
like me, you'll grow steady in grace
spread an arabesque of wings
and climb

each position one through five
stair steps to the sky?

that's right.

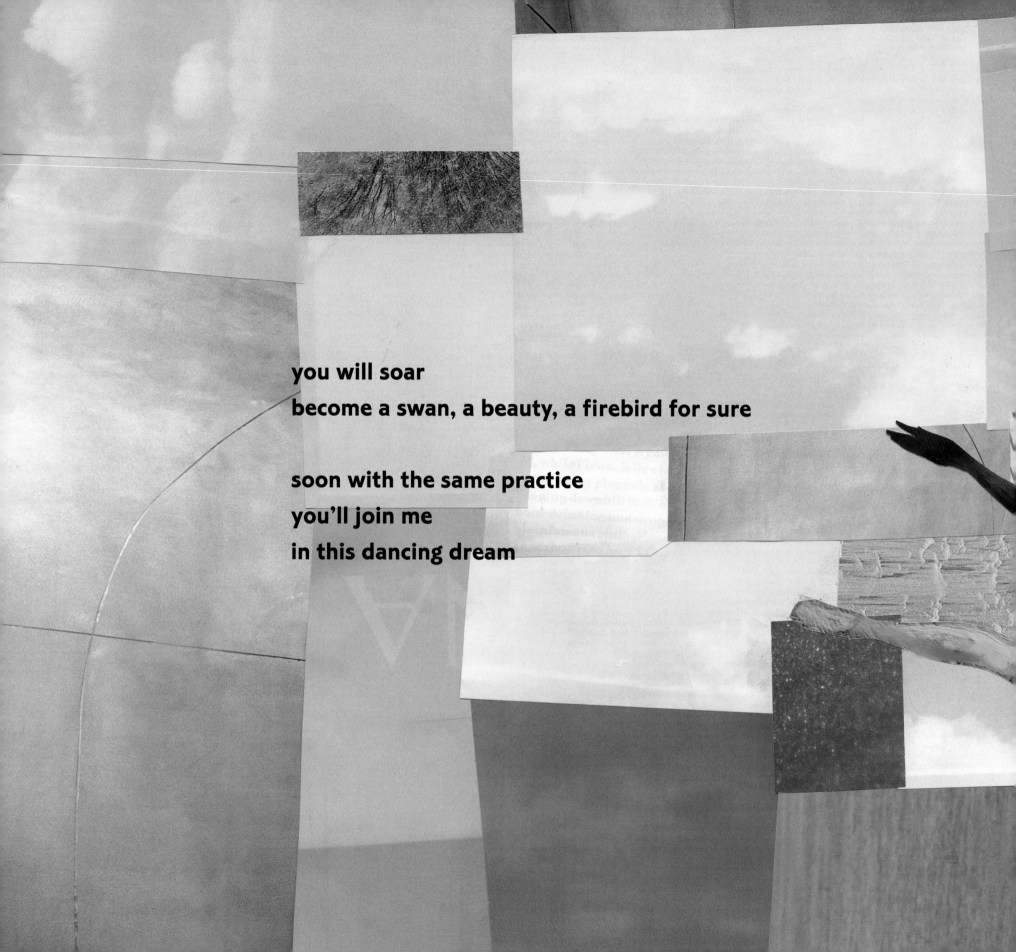

you will soar
become a swan, a beauty, a firebird for sure

soon with the same practice
you'll join me
in this dancing dream

in a pas de deux
a music box for two

we will wrap our hearts
careful as ribbons on pointe shoes

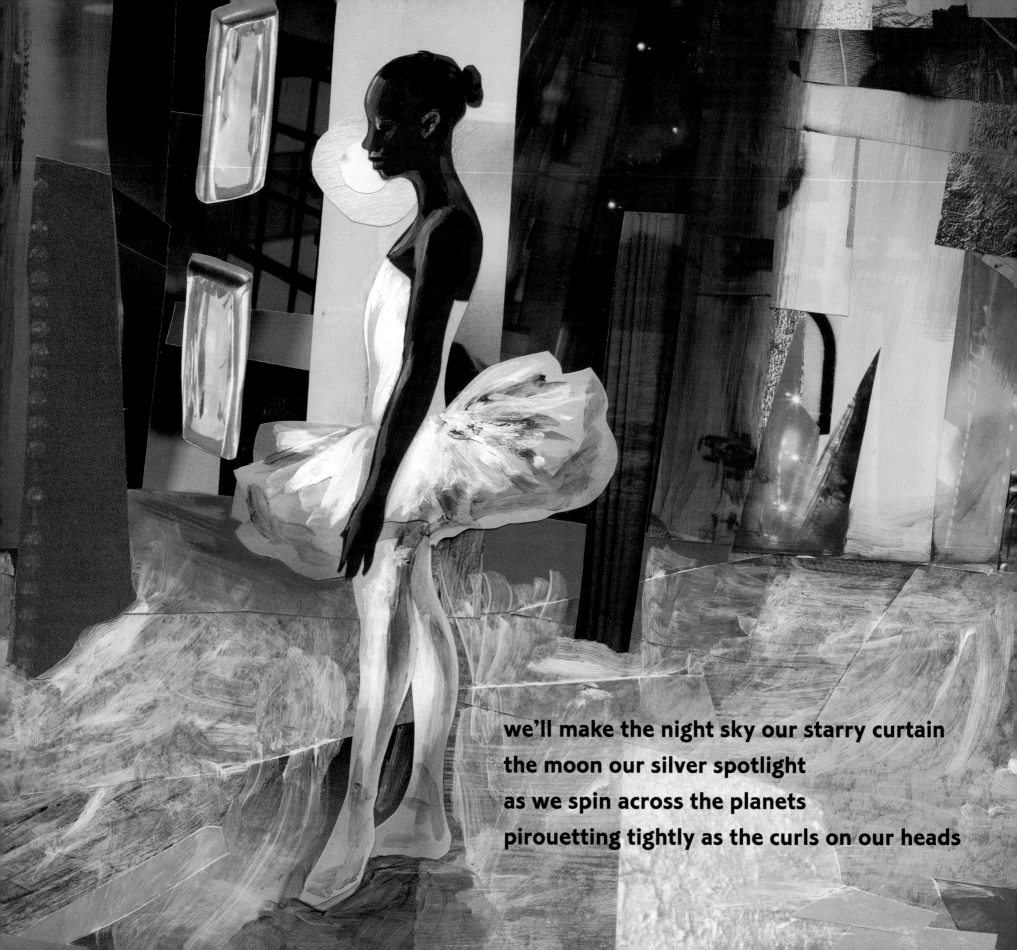

we'll make the night sky our starry curtain
the moon our silver spotlight
as we spin across the planets
pirouetting tightly as the curls on our heads

spinning wishes for new little ones
we can't yet imagine

then they will look to you in wonder
lighter than air and swift as
sunlight turning over the day
and say

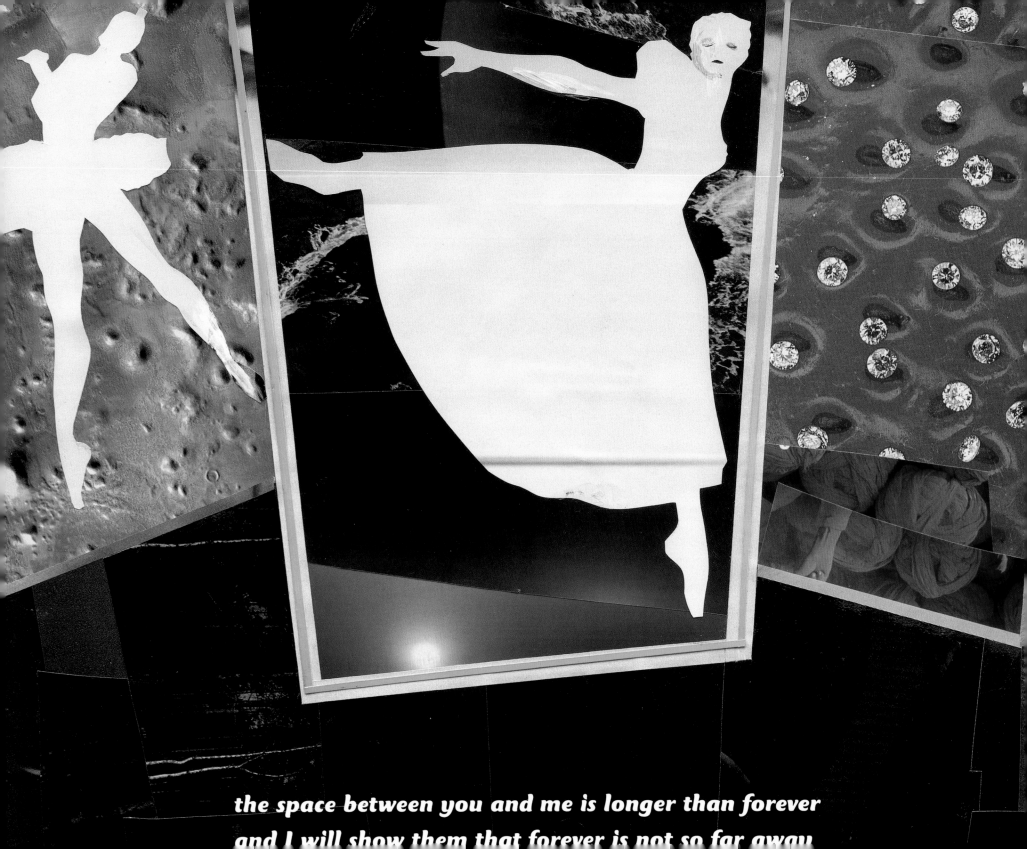

the space between you and me is longer than forever
and I will show them that forever is not so far away

© 2012 Gene Schiavone

Dear Reader,

I was once a little girl searching for my voice. Quiet, scared, unique, yet alive and vibrant. I struggled, caught among five siblings, desperate to be noticed. I never felt that I fit in anywhere. Not even at home surrounded by my family. My discovery of movement became my saving grace. When I was introduced to ballet, it was like finding the missing piece to my puzzle. I danced my worries and fears away.

The beauty of dance is being a part of something that is all you, from creation to performance. You hold the power of your instrument. That instrument comes in all shapes, sizes and colors. That instrument is your body, soul and heart. That instrument is you and me.

But when I opened up ballet books, I didn't see myself. I saw an image of what a ballerina should be, and she wasn't me, brown with tendrils sweeping her face. I needed to find ME. This book is you and me. I want to expand the idea of beauty and art.

Raven Wilkinson, African American ballerina with the Ballet Russe de Monte Carlo, and other amazing women took my hand and led me. Now it is my turn to lead others. This book is bringing my existence, and nonexistence as a young girl, to life, showing other girls and boys that they're not alone. They too can find their voice, their wings, their missing piece.

My hopes are that people will feel empowered to be whatever they want to be. To feel that they have no limits, just endless dreams that are reachable. No matter what that dream is, you have the power to make it come true with hard work and dedication, despite what you look like or struggle with.

I hope to pave a more definitive path than the one that was there for me but was just a little too hidden. I want to bring many with me to trace and create an even more vivid road to acceptance of yourself and from others.

Join me.

Sincerely yours,

Misty Copeland